Peter's 5 Railway Hits the Jackpot

Published by Christopher Vine 2013

Printed by The Amadeus Press
Cleckheaton, West Yorkshire,
England.

ISBN 978-0-9553359-9-0

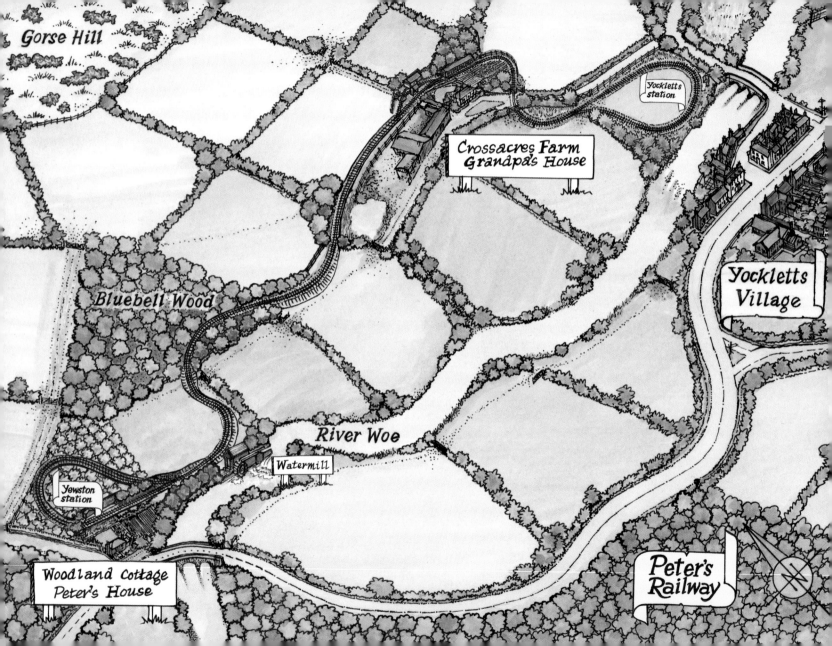

Gorse Hill

Yockletts station

Crossacres Farm
Grandpa's House

Yockletts
Village

Bluebell Wood

River Woe

Watermill

Yewston
station

Woodland Cottage
Peter's House

Peter's
Railway

The Peter's Railway Series

Over the last few years, Peter and his Grandpa have built a miniature steam railway across the farm. Originally it just linked their houses, but now it goes as far as Yockletts village where Peter goes to school. They've had plenty of thrills (and spills), but perhaps the biggest part of the fun has been building the railway. There is nothing in the world which is quite so satisfying as making something and then seeing it work for the first time.

The steam locomotive, Fiery Fox, belongs to Mr Esmond, but Peter and Grandpa have built everything else themselves: the track, the wagons and even the little buildings at the stations.

Last summer they built a watermill on the River Woe. It uses the power of the river to generate hydro-electricity, to run Crossacres Farm and Grandpa's house.

Peter and Grandpa have also made an engine themselves, Quicksilver, a small electric locomotive. This runs off a battery which gets charged at night using their free electricity. Quicksilver is useful because it's ready for work at the flick of a switch; whereas Fiery Fox takes a long time to prepare and get up steam.

Peter lives at Woodland Cottage, with his parents and the twins, Harry and Kitty. However, there is so much to do at Crossacres Farm that he spends almost all of his free time there, with Grandpa. The story in this book is their most ambitious adventure yet...

The watercolour illustrations are by John Wardle.

A big Rolls Royce crunched across the gravel drive.
But what was a large and expensive motor car doing at Crossacres Farm?
Grandpa had never owned a car, not even a small one.

It all started with... # The School Visit

Fiery Fox was simmering quietly at the little station by the river. The sun was shining, and steam from the chimney was drifting across the water. The children from Peter's school in Yockletts village were visiting the railway.

The visit had been organised by Peter's science teacher, Mr Hunter. Apart from being fun, it will be educational too. A steam engine is science and physics come to life, with nearly all the works on the outside so you can see and understand it. You can even see the coal releasing its energy as hot flames, making steam to move the train.

There were lots of passengers, so Peter and Grandpa had made the train as long as possible, using all of their wagons and carriages. Peter was on the engine, with Grandpa riding on the guard's van at the rear. The headmistress was sitting in the Granny Wagon, more politely known as Grandma's Special Saloon.

Having checked there was plenty of coal on the fire and water in the boiler, Peter was ready. "Hold on tight!" he called back to his friends on the train. "Enjoy the ride," he added as he released the brakes and opened the regulator.

Fiery Fox eased slowly forward and ran along the line beside the river. It was quite flat here and they built up speed rapidly.

"This is better than being at school!" the children shouted to each other, the wind blowing in their hair.

As the line turned away from the river, it started to climb across the field. Peter opened the regulator to work Fiery Fox harder. More steam rushed from the boiler into the cylinders, pushing the pistons back and forth, back and forth, turning the wheels and pulling the train up the steep gradient. Soon they were crossing the drive to the farm and running round behind Grandpa's house and through the farmyard beyond.

There was much to see. Animals, engine shed, turntable, duck pond and, of course, the lovely Highland cows in their field. One of the cows was standing on the track, so Peter gave a long, loud blast on the whistle. Grandpa's animals were quite used to having small steam trains running through their field, so the cow stepped lazily out of the way as the engine chuffed past.

A few minutes later, they arrived at the other end of the line, a mile from Yockletts village. Here was Woodland Cottage, the house where Peter lived. They didn't stop, but kept going round the loop and headed all the way back to Grandpa Gerald's house at Crossacres Farm.

"Did you enjoy the trip?" Peter asked when they had stopped.

"Yes!" everyone shouted at once, then off they went to explore the engine shed, the workshop and all the other things which make up a railway.

Peter and Grandpa showed them everything and tried to answer all of their questions, especially about how the engine worked.

Grandpa showed them how the coal burned, heating the water in the boiler to make steam.

"The boiler is incredibly strong. It has to be, to contain all the steam," he told them. "It can't escape, so it builds up to a great pressure. This high pressure steam is nothing like the steam you see coming out of a kettle. It contains lots of energy which can be used to force the pistons back and forwards in the cylinders."

"The pistons are a bit like your legs pushing the pedals on your bicycle," he explained.

Grandpa got them all to lie on the ground, right next to the track, while he drove the engine very slowly past them. They could see the piston rods pushing and pulling on the connecting rods, turning the wheels. Everything moved so smoothly and quietly.

"Would you like to see the engine go faster?" he asked them.

Of course they did, so Grandpa reversed back up the line, out of sight.

They heard the train approaching before they could see it. Suddenly it burst round a bend, going at an amazing speed. Steam, smoke and sparks were shooting out of the chimney with a roar. It was swaying from side to side as it rushed along the track.

Would it hold the rails?

Grandpa knew it was quite safe as he had been even faster before. But the children were alarmed and fascinated at the same time, as the engine shot past them.

It was a sensation of sight, sound and smell. Even the ground vibrated under the heavy engine. None of them dared to move until it had gone, then they all burst out laughing and chattering.

Mr Hunter was as thrilled as the children. "It's one thing teaching about science and engineering," he exclaimed. "But this is the laws of physics in action!"

"It's been fun showing you," replied Grandpa. "If you like our home-made science and engineering, jump back on the train and let me show you something else."

It was a pretty journey as they steamed down the line to Yockletts, then back through Bluebell Wood, across fields and through cuttings. Peter and Grandpa had made every bit of the railway themselves. Eventually the line swung back towards the river where Peter stopped at their watermill.

The watermill had been last summer's project. Some of the river water was diverted away from the waterfall, along a chute and fell onto a waterwheel, turning it slowly.

"What's it for?" asked one of the children.

Grandpa pointed at the water running down the chute. "The energy in the water, instead of being wasted as it falls down the waterfall," he explained, "is converted by the waterwheel into useful mechanical energy, which drives an electric generator."

"It produces enough electricity to power the farm, my house and keeps Quicksilver charged up; all completely free."

Peter, who was rightly proud of what they had built together, opened the door of the little mill building, so they could see the machinery inside. Pulleys and belts were driving the generator with a soft humming noise. "There's an underground cable," he pointed out, "which takes the power to the farm and house."

They enjoyed watching the wheels go round and asked lots of questions. But soon it was time for Peter to drive his friends back to school.

The children all thanked Grandpa for taking the time to show them his wonderful railway. "I enjoyed showing it to you," he beamed. "I hope you will all come and visit again, maybe in the holidays. You could bring picnics to eat beside the river."

Back at school, they were all discussing their visit. "Wouldn't it be fun," asked Mr Hunter, "if we could take a train to school every day?"

They all agreed of course. It would be much more exciting too!

"And with all that fresh air, you would be wide awake by the time you arrived," added Mr Hunter laughing.

"I think we will have to try to persuade Peter and his Grandpa to extend the line. It will make a brilliant project for geography, science and maths lessons."

"Let's get started right now," he decided. "We need to do some calculations!"

Grandpa goes to School

A couple of weeks after the visit, Grandpa received a letter. It was from Mr Hunter, inviting him to Peter's school. "The children have been working on a project and they would like to show it to you," the letter said.

At the next assembly, Grandpa found himself sitting in the front row.

"Since our visit to your railway, the children have been very busy," began Mr Hunter. "They have done some calculations and the results will surprise you. I will let the class tell you about it themselves."

With the help of a diagram, the youngsters explained how much fuel was used to bring children to school from Oaksted village.

They explained that there were 37 children who came by car from Oaksted, 8 miles away. They talked Grandpa through all their calculations and told him that every year, the distance travelled by cars on the school run was an incredible 228,000 miles.

"Goodness gracious!" exclaimed Grandpa when a crazy thought jumped into his head. "That's as far as the Moon."

The children then estimated that most cars would do about 10 miles for every litre of fuel. The amount of fuel used worked out at 22,800 litres - an unbelievable amount of petrol or diesel!!! They had done one last calculation to show that the fuel used would fill a small swimming pool.

"It's a terrible waste of fuel, and think of all the pollution," they told Grandpa, before asking him a question.

"Would you please consider extending your railway, so the children who live in Oaksted can come to school by train?"

How much fuel is used bringing children to school from Oaksted?

37 children come from Oaksted by car

8 miles to school on morning run →

Cars go home without children ←

8 miles to pick up on afternoon run →

Cars go home with children ←

Each car does 4 x 8 miles = 32 miles every day

With 37 cars, that is 37 x 32 miles = approx 1200 miles per day.

There are 190 school days in a year

So the total distance travelled by cars on the school run from Oaksted is 1200 miles x 190 = 228,000 miles per year

Modern cars travel about 10 miles using 1 litre of fuel

So the fuel used is 228,000 divided by 10 = 22,800 litres per year

That converts to 22.8 or approx 23 cubic metres.

A small swimming pool might be 5 metres long, by 4 metres wide and 1 metre deep. Its volume would be 5 x 4 x 1 cubic metres = 20 cubic metres. That's about the same as the fuel used.

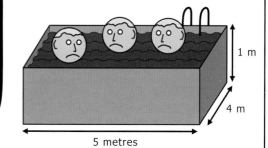

1 m

4 m

5 metres

These calculations are only very approximate. You might call them an 'order of magnitude' calculation.

Grandpa had been listening carefully and was astonished. "This is a serious problem," he agreed. "You are right, something must be done. It's just a question of what and how."

"Quite apart from the question of how we might pay for it, I think we would also have to consider what type of train to use."

"The problem with using Fiery Fox," he continued, "is that it takes over an hour to get up steam. If Peter were to run a steam train every morning, he would have to get up very early to be ready in time!"

"What about using a diesel engine?" one of the children suggested. "You could start that up in a few seconds."

Grandpa agreed that it could be started up quickly. The problem was that diesel fuel would still be expensive and polluting.

Another of the children suggested building an electric train and powering it from the watermill.

Everyone agreed this was a brilliant plan, but Grandpa had a tricky question.

"How do you suggest we get the electricity to the train?" he asked with a twinkle in his eye.

"An overhead wire, just like the real railways," shouted out one boy. "The electric engine would have a pantograph on top, to pick up the electricity from the wire."

"Can anyone see a problem with that idea?" asked Mr Hunter.

"We will all get electric shocks if it touches our heads," one of the girls pointed out. "And your hair would stand on end!" laughed one of the boys.

"What about a 3rd rail for the electricity, like they use on the railways in the South of England?" suggested another pupil.

Grandpa didn't like the sound of that idea at all. "Are you trying to electrocute my cows?" he chuckled.

It was Peter who had the solution to their problem. "Could we make the train operate from a battery, and then charge it up at night, using the watermill electricity?" he asked. "Like we do with our little electric engine, Quicksilver."

"It's a good idea," Grandpa agreed. "A few tractor batteries should be plenty big enough to run a couple of trips a day. And we don't have much use for the electricity at night, so it really will be free."

"Mind you," he added, "we haven't worked out how to pay for the extra line yet. It's five miles across the fields to Oaksted from Woodland Cottage and I don't even own the land. There are a lot of problems to overcome."

"Meanwhile, perhaps I should tell you the story about an English train driver in France."

"He was driving a Eurostar train from London to Paris," began Grandpa. "He had already gone through the Channel Tunnel and was now speeding through France at 186 miles an hour, when he saw a large male deer, or stag, on the line."

"It jumped out of the way in time, but the driver wanted to report it to the control room by radio. The only problem was that he didn't know the French word for a deer or stag."

"Luckily though, he did know the word for cow - 'vache', so with a bit of cunning he told the controller that, on the line there was a 'vache avec pantograph' - a cow with a pantograph!"

It was such a bad joke that everyone laughed. But Mr Hunter soon brought the party back to order. "Thank you for listening," he said to Grandpa. "I know it would be a huge undertaking to extend the line, but will you consider it?"

"Of course I will," replied Grandpa. "And I think the calculations you have done are most interesting. It is just the sheer cost of five miles of line. Let me think about it for a few days..."

And with that, he went home.

Electric Railway
How to get the electricity to the train

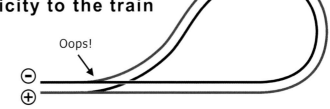

Oops!

Model Railway - Two rail supply
In a typical electric model railway, the electricity is supplied by two wires to the two rails. The motor in the loco picks up the electricity through the metal wheels.

A major problem with two rail electricity supply
Many types of junctions on a railway would not work. This turning loop has a supply to the two rails. Follow the positive (red) side round the loop and it joins onto the negative (black) side. Effectively the two wires have been crossed to make a 'short circuit', this would blow a fuse!

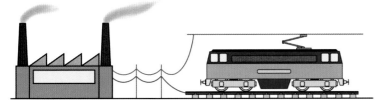

Overhead wire and pantograph
Most full size railways today use an overhead wire (red) to supply electricity to the train. The electricity is picked up from the wire by a pantograph (pink) and returned to the power station, through the wheels and the metal rails (blue).

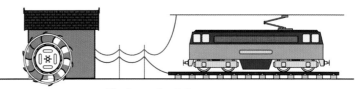

Hydro-electric power
Most electricity in the world is generated in power stations which burn coal, oil or gas. However some countries, like Switzerland and Norway, are lucky and have lots of rivers and mountains to generate hydro-electricity. This makes no pollution.

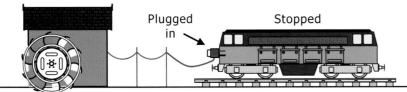

Plugged in

Stopped

Battery powered locomotive - plugged in to the watermill
The batteries (pink) are low on charge and are being recharged using hydro-electricity from the watermill. This creates no pollution and emits no carbon dioxide gas into the atmosphere. The train cannot go anywhere because the cable would be snapped or the plug pulled out!

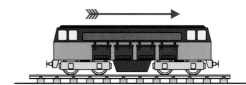

Loco running using electricity from batteries
The loco is now unplugged and running from the fully charged (red) batteries. Battery power is not much use in full size trains, because the batteries cannot hold enough charge (energy) to work all day.

Help!

"It's a brilliant idea," Grandpa told Grandma later. "I'm full of admiration for what they have worked out, but it will be just so expensive."

"Why don't you ask the government to pay for it?" she suggested. "Your scheme seems quite sensible compared to some of the projects they pay for with public money."

"Look at this," she continued, warming to her subject. "The government are to spend a million pounds for prisoners to go on trips to the zoo!" she read from her newspaper. "Anyone would think they had money to burn."

"Why don't you write to the Minister of Transport and explain your railway to him? You should tell him how much fuel it will save and how it will put absolutely no carbon dioxide gas into the atmosphere. With your plan to run the train on our hydro-electricity, it would be the greenest and least polluting transport system in the country."

Peter, who was listening, added to the idea. "We've got all the surveys which the parents filled in for the school project. They would show him that the railway would be fully used, if we built it. It isn't just a dream."

So Peter and Grandpa sat down to write a letter. There were lots of things to put in, but they didn't want it to be long-winded and muddled. It had to be clear and to the point.

"At the beginning, we need to tell him that this is a real problem with a real solution," suggested Grandpa.

"And we need to tell him about our hydro-electric generator, which will power the trains, without any diesel or petrol being burnt at all," added Peter. "He will see that we can help to reduce pollution caused by transport."

"You need to tell him about the railway you have already built," added Grandma. "Put some pictures in with the letter to show that you really can do this. Otherwise he might just think you're bonkers!"

It took them hours. Which bit should go first, how should it finish? Then it was too long, so they cut bits out and wrote some parts differently. At last they thought it was beginning to make sense, so they gave it to Grandma to read.

"I think it's very good," she said after a few minutes. "But you need to finish it really strongly by asking him for some money to pay for it all, and making it clear that this is an opportunity for him to do something fantastic."

"You might add that he will be invited to open the line. He will have his picture in all the newspapers with lots of happy children on the train. Politicians just love that sort of thing!" she grinned, handing back the letter.

"Just don't get your hopes up too much. Getting a straight answer from a politician is like trying to nail jelly to a wall!" she added helpfully, with one of her funny sayings.

An hour later, with the letter finished, Peter signed it and Grandma promised to post it in the morning.

Can the Railway be Built?

For the next few days, the talk at Crossacres Farm was of nothing else but the new railway. Peter was desperate to build it, but Grandpa worried about the expense. He also knew it was very unlikely that the Minister of Transport would ever help them.

"We will need to build the line across other farms," said Grandpa thoughtfully. "We don't even know if the farmers will let us use their land."

"The first thing to do is to walk the route from Woodland Cottage to Oaksted, and see where the line would run - a sort of preliminary survey. When shall we do it?"

"Well I don't know about you," grinned Peter, "but I've got energy bursting from every pore. Let's get going!"

"We can get Quicksilver out and take the train down to my house," he said while pulling on his coat. "We can walk from there."

"It's a good thing we made this little electric locomotive," Grandpa smiled, as they

opened the engine shed door. "Although Fiery Fox is a wonderful machine, it does take ages getting up steam."

Quicksilver was ready to go in an instant, so they set off across the fields, down the line to Woodland Cottage. The little electric engine wasn't fast, but it was much quicker than walking.

Even more satisfying was that the little loco and the watermill had been built, almost entirely, out of scrap bits and pieces which were lying about the farm.

It was an enjoyable run along the line. The duck pond whizzed by, then Bluebell Wood, animals, the river and their waterwheel turning slowly. They were scooting across the fields, powered by water which had been turning the waterwheel last night. Some of the hydro-electricity had been used to charge the engine's battery.

At the far end of the line they stopped and had a careful look at where the new line could head off across the fields, on its way to Oaksted.

"This first field belongs to me," pointed out Grandpa, "which means we can run the line where we like. After that though, it will have to go on land which belongs to our neighbours."

"We'll have to ask them if we could buy a thin strip of land, along the edges of their fields. We don't want to interfere with their farming too much."

Grandpa took an old envelope and a pen from his jacket pocket, and handed them to Peter. "You sketch a map as we walk, of where the line might go."

Before they had gone a hundred metres, they came upon the first major obstacle. The bottom part of Gorse Hill ran across the field, blocking the route.

"I had never realised how hilly this field is," observed Grandpa. "Gorse Hill is too steep to go over, and we can't go round it because that will send the line in the wrong direction."

Peter didn't see this as a problem of course. It was the perfect excuse for a tunnel!

"You're right," agreed Grandpa. "And apart from the fun of having a tunnel to run through, I think we can turn a major difficulty into an opportunity at the same time."

"We're going to need somewhere to store the new electric train. If we fit doors at the ends of the tunnel, it will make a perfect train shed."

"It's right next to my house too," added Peter. "I won't have far to walk to get to the train in the mornings."

With the tunnel agreed, at least in principle, they set off on foot to Oaksted, making notes and sketches as they went. Staying close to the edges of the fields, they found that the ground was almost perfectly level. They would need a few small cuttings and embankments, but nothing which Grandpa's old digger couldn't manage.

Then they came to a slightly bigger problem, the River Wye. This was a small tributary to the River Woe and there was no way round it.

"Now it's my turn for some fun!" laughed Grandpa. "You always wanted a tunnel on the line, and I've always wanted a bridge. The Oaksted extension is going to be a grand spectacle!"

"We can have a lot of fun designing it all," he added. "Don't forget though, this project is still just a pipe-dream. We haven't got the money to build it yet and we still haven't worked out where we could put the station at Oaksted."

And so they tramped on, until they reached the village.

It was a pretty place which time seemed to have forgotten. The railway station was right on the edge, with some really old timber-framed houses on one side of the line, and fields on the other.

This was perfect, as our two surveyors could run their new line right up to the mainline station. Passengers would be able to transfer from the full size trains to the small ones, and Peter's Railway would become a 'through route' to Yockletts.

Over the next few weeks, the two railway promoters made drawings and maps for the project. Aside from the lack of money, there was also a vital question. Would the farmers allow them to use their land?

One Sunday afternoon, Peter and Grandpa set off on foot, crossing the fields to Wadden Farm. They were going to call on their neighbour to discuss the railway.

Minnie the dog came with them, darting off ahead and sniffing out interesting smells, sticks, and then more smells.

As they approached the farmhouse, Moss the Black Labrador came out to greet them. Moss was a great friend of Minnie's and there was much wagging of tails and barking as they said hello. Mr Izard appeared at the door to see what all the commotion was about.

"Come on in!" he called, when he saw his neighbours. "To what do I owe the pleasure of this visit?"

Grandpa and Peter explained all about their proposed extension of the line, how useful it would be, and the pollution it would prevent.

"We were wondering," Peter asked, "if you would consider selling a strip of land for the line?"

After a long pause, during which Peter could hear his heart bumping, Mr Izard smiled and said it was a brilliant idea. "Let's go out right now," he suggested, "and walk the route."

"You show me the strip you need and we'll agree a fair price for it. Then I'll walk on with you to Bean Farm where we can talk to Mr Coni. If we all go together, he'll see what a good plan it is and I am sure he will be agreeable too."

They explained the scheme to Mr Coni, who looked very serious. "I might consider it," he said carefully. "But there is one condition..."

"My little boy, Edward, is four now," he continued, "and very soon he'll be starting at your school. I'll sell you the strip of land if you promise to build a little platform so Edward can go on the train too."

What a relief! Of course they would provide a station for Edward.

After some serious discussion, the three farmers agreed a price for the land.

Peter was so excited he could hardly contain himself. "Now we can build the line!" he said, jumping up and down. He could already imagine trains rushing across miles of farmland.

"Steady on Peter!" said Grandpa cautiously. "Don't forget, we still don't know how to pay for it..."

Ridgeway Tunnel

Garse Hill

Crossacres Farm
Grandpa's House

Yockletts
School

Yockletts

Oaksted Extension

River Woe

Nature
Reserve

Watermill

Woodland Cottage
Peter's House

Square Cubes

Four weeks had gone by and Peter was beginning to give up hope of ever getting a reply from the Minister. But one day, the postman delivered an important looking letter.

Grandpa wanted to open it, but waited until Peter could drop by after school.

When he arrived, Peter opened the letter with trembling hands and read it out loud:

Dear Peter,

Thank you for your most interesting letter. It is not very often that I receive requests for funding a new railway line, especially from a schoolboy!

However, what you propose is eminently sensible and I can see that you have given it a lot of careful thought. I can also see that your hydro-electric powered line will save a lot of atmospheric pollution and, here at the Ministry of Transport, that is my number one priority.

But....

"Oh dear," said Grandma, "I think he's going to turn you down."

Peter carried on reading:

> The trouble with railways is that they are just
> so expensive to build and my department is
> operating on a very tight budget this year.

"That means he hasn't got any money," added Grandma gloomily.

> Indeed, the last new stretch of railway we built
> cost £82 million for a 10 mile line. That works
> out at over £8 million per mile. At 5 miles long,
> the new Oaksted line would cost £40 million, a
> sum which we simply cannot afford to pay.

> However, I note that your proposal is for a
> miniature railway, one eighth of full size and so
> should cost only an eighth as much. If the
> Ministry of Transport agreed to pay £1 million
> per mile, would that be sufficient to construct
> the line?

"A m..m..million p..pounds a mile!" spluttered Grandpa. "He's crazy!"

"That's five million pounds for the whole line," said Peter, sitting down. Then he leapt out of the chair and started jumping up and down.

"We can build the line! We're RICH!!"

"There must be some mistake," said Grandma, rather more calmly than the others. "Read the rest of the letter and make sure you've not misunderstood it."

Peter carried on reading:

There are two conditions which are attached to this offer:

1. You must guarantee to me that you will not come back and ask for any more money to help pay for the running costs of the line. The big railway companies are always doing this, and it costs me a fortune.

2. The railway must be finished by the end of the summer holidays, ready for the start of school term. In September I am appearing on TV in a programme about saving the planet through modern transport, and I want to be able to talk about the success of your project and show the line in action!

Subject to the above conditions, The Ministry of Transport agrees to pay up to £5 million for the 5 mile extension of your miniature railway from Woodland Cottage to the village of Oaksted.

I remain your humble and obedient servant,
Ian M A Pratt
Minister of Transport

After a few moments of stunned silence, they all jumped up, cheering and hugging each other.

"Not only are we going to get £5 million to build the line," laughed Peter, "but we're going to be on telly as well!"

Grandma was tickled pink. "Oooh, you could knock me down with a feather," she giggled. (That was another of Grandma's funny sayings.) "I'll have to buy a new hat."

When they had all calmed down a little, Grandpa explained that the Minister clearly was not an engineer or a mathematician.

"He has made a very simple and obvious mistake," he grinned. "He doesn't understand the elementary mathematics of squares and cubes. I'll explain it all to you later, with some diagrams..."

"But now it's time for a celebration," he announced. "Let's have a cup of tea!"

However, there was something that Peter and his grandparents did not know. Back at the Ministry of Transport, Mr Pratt did not think for one moment that they would ever build the line. He would never have to pay for it.

'They'll never manage to build it in time,' he had thought to himself. 'And the farmers along the route will never sell their land.'

He had chuckled quietly as he had signed the letter and put it in his out-tray for posting. 'But at least I haven't said "no". That would never do...'

Squares and Area
Why did the Minister offer to pay too much?

Squares

In maths, if you multiply a number by itself it becomes a 'Square'. Examples are 2 x 2 = 4 or 3 x 3 = 9 or 4 x 4 = 16

A simple drawing shows why these numbers are called
Squares or square numbers

 ↕ 1 cm

↔ 1 cm

 2 cm

2 cm

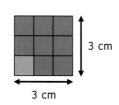 3 cm

3 cm

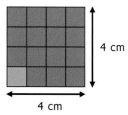 4 cm

4 cm

This little square has sides
1 centimetre long.
It covers an **area** of
1 square centimetre.
(cm is short for centimetre.)

This square is twice as big
but has an area
4 times as big.
(count the little squares.)

This square is 3 times as big
but has an area
9 times as big
(count the little squares.)

4 times larger and 16 times the area!
The area of the large square is
4 cm x 4 cm = 16 square cm
(The area is the 'square' of the sides.)

The Minister has offered to pay one eighth of what it costs to build a full size railway, because Peter's Railway is 8 times smaller than full size. But this is wrong!

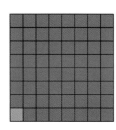

PR size   Full size (x 8)

Peter's Railway is 8 times **smaller**
(in both height **and** width) than full size,
so the area of everything is
8 x 8 = 64 times smaller.
But why is this important?

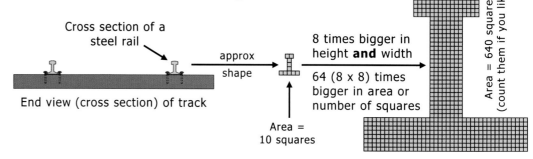

Cross section of a
steel rail

End view (cross section) of track

approx
shape

8 times bigger in
height **and** width

64 (8 x 8) times
bigger in area or
number of squares

Area =
10 squares

Area = 640 squares
(count them if you like!)

These two pictures show the end or 'cross section' of a piece of steel rail, one is
8 times smaller than the other. However the cross sectional **area** of the smaller rail
is 64 times smaller. So in a length of mini rail, there is 64 times less steel. The mini
rail would be something like 64 times cheaper, not 8 times cheaper.
The Minister has offered to pay 8 times too much!

(It is 8 times too much because he is paying 8 times less when the materials
will cost 64 times less. 64 divided by 8 = 8)

Cubes, Volume and Weight

Cubes

How about multiplying a number by itself three times to obtain its 'Cube'? EG 2 x 2 x 2 = 8 or 3 x 3 x 3 = 27
Again a simple drawing makes it easy to understand why these numbers are called Cubes.

1 cm

This little cube has sides 1 cm long.
(1 cm wide, 1 cm high and 1 cm deep)
It occupies a **volume** of
1 cubic centimetre (1 cc).

2 cm

This cube is twice as big
but has a volume of 8 cubic cm
It is also shown 'exploded' so you can
count the little cubes.

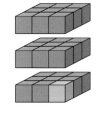

3 cm

3 times larger and 27 times the volume!
The volume of the cube is
3 cm x 3 cm x 3 cm = 27 cubic cm
(The volume is the 'cube' of the sides.)

It is amazing how big numbers become when you square or cube them. The square of 10 is 100 and the cube of 10 is 1000!

Exploded view ⟶
so you can count the little
cubes!! (there are 512)

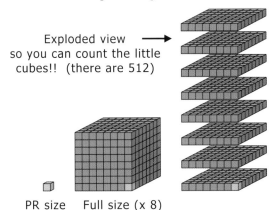

PR size   Full size (x 8)

Peter's Railway is 8 times smaller
(in height **and** width **and** depth) than full size,
so the volume of everything is
8 x 8 x 8 = 512 times smaller.
This is even more important.

These pictures show two locomotives, one is 8 times smaller than the other in length. However the volume of (or amount of steel in) the smaller engine is 512 times smaller. So the cost of the steel and other materials would be about 512 times less than full size.

The miniature engine also weighs about 512 times less than the big one.

For the train, the Minister has offered to pay 64 times too much!

(It is 64 times too much because he is paying 8 times less when the materials
will cost 512 times less. 512 divided by 8 = 64)

PR Construction Limited

Once they had recovered from the shock and excitement of the Minister's letter, Grandpa made a decision.

"This project is going to be enormous," he began. "Much bigger than anything we have done before."

"There's no way we can make and do everything ourselves. Quite apart from the length of the line, there is the problem of finishing it so quickly. If we miss the deadline, we won't get the money!"

"This time we are going to have to get outside help, from professional contractors and engineering firms," he decided. "We'll need to start a limited company."

"Whatever will you call it?" asked Grandma. "Rip-Off Railways Limited?"

"Certainly not," said Peter indignantly. "I think we'll call it 'PR Construction Limited.' That sounds like a proper firm."

"Excellent," agreed Grandpa. "*PR Construction* it shall be. Tomorrow morning we'll register the name with Companies House and then we can go into the bank to open a new bank account. That will keep all the money for the railway quite separate."

"You two are going to have plenty to do," observed Grandma. "So I'll do all the book-keeping for the company," she offered. "You can put my name down as the official Company Secretary. I'll take care of the paperwork."

This was in fact a very generous offer from Grandma. It was going to take her a lot of time and would let Peter and Grandpa devote all their efforts to designing and managing the railway construction. But where to start?

They sat down with a blank sheet of paper and started to make notes of the things they would have to do.

"There's just one fly in the ointment," said Grandma (who must have been swotting up on funny sayings). "You won't get the money until the line is finished. That is what the Minister said in his letter. How are you going to buy the land and get all these companies working for you, if you can't pay them?"

"Don't worry about that," replied Grandpa. "I know just how to do it."

"We will ask them to quote a price for their work, and to include the fact that we will be paying them a month or so after the line is complete."

"They will add a bit onto their prices," he explained. "But with £5 million, that won't worry us!"

With that happy thought, they began to jot down a list of all the things they would need for the new railway.

List of things needed

1. Land. Luckily in the five miles to Oaksted there were only two farms. One was owned by Mr Mark Izard, the other by Mr F Coni. The sale was already agreed.

2. Track material for 5 miles or 8000 metres.

> Rails. 5 miles of track with 2 rails = 10 miles or 16,000 metres.
>
> Sleepers. 8000 metres of track with 5 sleepers per metre = 40,000.
>
> Screws to hold rails to sleepers. 4 screws per sleeper = 160,000.
>
> Ballast stones. 25 kilograms per metre of track = 200,000 kg or 200 tonnes.
>
> Points for the junction with the old line and any sidings.

3. Material for a tunnel. Design to follow. (Power supply for charging batteries.)

4. Material for a bridge. Design to follow.

5. A new electric train. Design to follow.

6. Fencing to keep the new line separate from the farmland and animals.

7. A building firm who could provide men and machines to build the line.

8. An engineering firm who could make all the special parts, engine, carriages, etc...

"It's a long list and a vast amount of material," noted Grandpa when they had finished. "Seeing it written down on paper makes me realise just what a giant undertaking this is."

"I know," grinned Peter, "But with £5 million to spend, it's not going to be a problem. Nothing can stop the Oaksted Line!"

"Just remember Peter," Grandma warned him. "Don't count your chickens before they've hatched."

That night, Peter fell asleep dreaming of starting a global construction company...

Mass Production

Just one week before the end of term, all the contracts had been agreed for supplying equipment and building the line. School was finishing on Friday afternoon and work could start on Monday morning.

The route had already been marked out with wooden posts and most of the material had been delivered. In the yard outside were stacks of rails, a mountain of ballast stones, boxes of screws, tins of paint, fencing material and more.

During the week, Mr Beer and his two brothers delivered two large diggers and a telescopic loader. They were going to dig out the track bed, cuttings and embankments.

Finally, towering over everything else, was a massive stack of sleepers, 40,000 of them, stacked up like a giant game of Jenga! They had been supplied by their old friend, Mr Plank from the sawmill.

"Here they come!" called Peter to Grandpa. It was 8 o'clock on Monday morning, and lorries and vans were driving up the road.

"Good morning everybody, and great to see you," Grandpa greeted them. "I know you've all got plans and drawings to work from, but if anything isn't clear, please just ask. We don't have time to do the job twice."

The Beer brothers set off across the fields in their diggers, while Mr Jackson and his fencing team picked up piles of wooden posts and wire, and went off to Bean Farm.

Then a minibus arrived in the yard, driven by Mr Hunter, with ten of Peter's friends from school. They wanted to help build the railway and had volunteered to assemble the track sections, or panels, all 2,600 of them...

One of the boys, William, looked at the monster stack of sleepers. "Wow!" he said. "We'll never get all those done. That's a job for a factory."

"Don't panic," smiled Grandpa. "Peter and I have made you some jigs, to help with the assembly. If you form into five teams, you'll have the job done easily."

He showed them the boards they had made, with pegs to locate the sleepers and rails. "All you have to do is set 15 sleepers on the board and the two rails on top. Then you just put in the 60 screws with electric screwdrivers."

The youngsters looked a bit doubtful, so he carried on. "I reckon each panel will take 15 minutes to assemble, so if you stick at it for 5 hours a day, with 5 teams, you will have made all 2,600 of them in 26 days. Less than a month. Easy!"

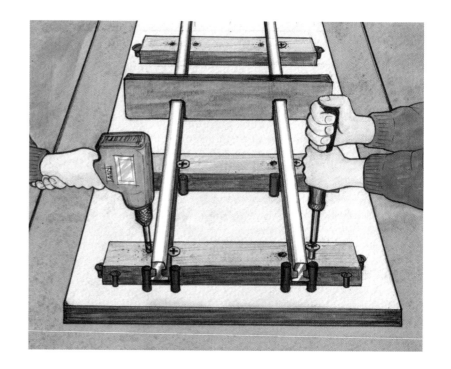

Luckily at this moment Grandma came out. "Don't worry," she said, seeing their faces. "I'll bring out snacks, drinks and huge lunches of energy-filled sandwiches."

It didn't take long to get the hang of it, and soon they were stacking up the finished track panels. It became a competition, with each team trying to make the most.

Naughty William sneaked off one afternoon, from the hard work. The other children were just about to go and find him, when Grandma arrived with piles of food and drink. Never mind about William, they demolished the whole lot without him!

Meanwhile, out in the fields, the men and machines were busy preparing the ground and shovelling ballast stones with the loader. As fast as the children finished the track, another team of men was taking it away to be laid and levelled on the ballast. Maybe they were having a competition too...

One morning the telephone rang and Grandma handed it to Grandpa. "It's the lady from Four Mile House," she whispered. "You'd better talk to her and calm her down if you can. She's in a terrible stew; something about the noise. Diggers, hammering, that sort of thing."

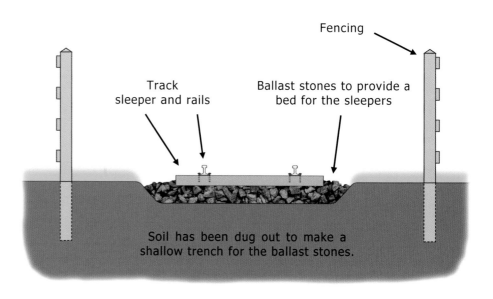

Cross section view of the line construction.

Fencing

Track sleeper and rails

Ballast stones to provide a bed for the sleepers

Soil has been dug out to make a shallow trench for the ballast stones.

"..... I am sorry Mrs Smith," said Grandpa when he could get a word in. "But I promise that the noise outside your house will be finished by the end of today."

"Perhaps I could offer to pay for you and your husband to go out for a long lunch while we finish that stretch of line. Would that help?"

Grandpa winked at Peter, while still holding the phone away from his ear. Mrs Smith was still complaining, but she was running out of steam at last.

"Thank goodness for that!" said Grandpa when he'd put the phone down. "We didn't want a re-enactment of the Battle of Skelmanthorpe."

Peter and Grandma had never heard of Skelmanthorpe before, and certainly didn't know about any battle there. So Grandpa explained.

"In the year of 1874," he began, "the Lancashire & Yorkshire Railway was building a line near the village of Skelmanthorpe. One day the navvies, who were digging a cutting, went into the village and had a wild party. In fact they made a real nuisance of themselves."

"The villagers were so cross that, later on, they went out and dropped rocks on the navvies, from the top of the cutting!"

"As you can imagine, that started a pretty serious fight," laughed Grandpa. "I didn't fancy Mrs Smith trying the same thing on us!"

With the Battle of Oaksted narrowly averted, work carried on. In the yard, the piles of sleepers, rails and ballast got smaller, and the line grew longer.

Peter had taken to using Quicksilver to get home to Woodland Cottage, in the evenings. Then he could use it in the morning, to get back up to the farm.

"Don't forget to put the battery on charge," called Grandpa after him, as he whizzed off down the line, into the dusk. "Unless you want to walk…"

It was a lovely journey after a long day's work, and this was the perfect way to relax. Quicksilver, the engine they had made, humming along the line they had built. Crossing a field, now weaving through Bluebell Wood, then running along beside the river.

All on his own.

Peter found himself humming too. Life was good!

The Tunnel of Gloom

Grandpa was out with Peter, checking progress on the line.

"The teams are getting on well," he observed. "I reckon they must have built a mile of track."

"But now it's time for us to get stuck into our tunnel project, through Gorse Hill. But not literally stuck in!" he added quickly.

"How are we going to make it?" asked Peter. "We don't have a tunnelling machine and it'll take forever to dig it out with spades."

"If the tunnel isn't too deep underground," explained Grandpa, "there's a cunning method, called 'Cut and Cover'."

"We can dig a deep trench, then lower in a large pipe to make a ready-made tunnel. Then we can use the digger to push all the soil back in, to cover it up."

"In a few months, the grass will have grown back and it will look fine again."

Peter wanted to know where they would get the pipes from.

"Drainage companies stock all sorts of pipes," replied Grandpa. "They're used to divert small streams and rainwater, and can be made from plastic, metal or concrete."

"Once we have worked out the size we need," he continued, "they will advise us on which sort of pipe is strong enough to support the ground above it."

Back at the farm, they began to think about the height of the tunnel.

"It would look really good," started Peter, "if it was the correct scale size for our one-eighth size trains. But we'll bang our heads unless we all lie flat on the wagons!"

"Yes," agreed Grandpa. "We would certainly get complaints about that."

Out in the engine shed, Peter sat on a wagon, while Grandpa measured how high he could reach.

"I think we had better make it a bit higher than that," decided Peter. "We need to make it big enough for Grandma's saloon carriage. Otherwise there will be a bit of a smash-up when we try to take her for a trip to Oaksted!"

"You're right, of course," said Grandpa grimacing. He still hadn't forgotten the last time there was an accident with the Granny Wagon (with Granny in it, unfortunately!).

Once they had worked out the size of the pipe, they returned to Gorse Hill to measure its length. Their wooden stakes showed the exact route the line would follow.

Walking over the top, they measured the distance between each stake and added them up. 82 metres long and on a curve too. "It's going to be quite some tunnel," observed Grandpa. "There will be a lot of digging and hard work."

"It's going to be fantastic," added Peter with a grin. "Completely dark in the middle and, because of the curves, you won't be able to see all the way through."

"There's one extra complication," he realised. "If we're going to use the tunnel to store the new electric train, it will be blocked. We won't be able to drive Fiery Fox up the new line to Oaksted."

"We'll need to build a siding somewhere to put it out of the way, clear of the tunnel."

"Let's do a proper drawing tonight," Grandpa suggested, "and I'll get everything ordered up in the morning."

The next day, with concrete pipes and bricks ordered, they could get started on digging out the trench for the tunnel. The pipes were very expensive, but luckily they still wouldn't make much of a dent in the £5 million!

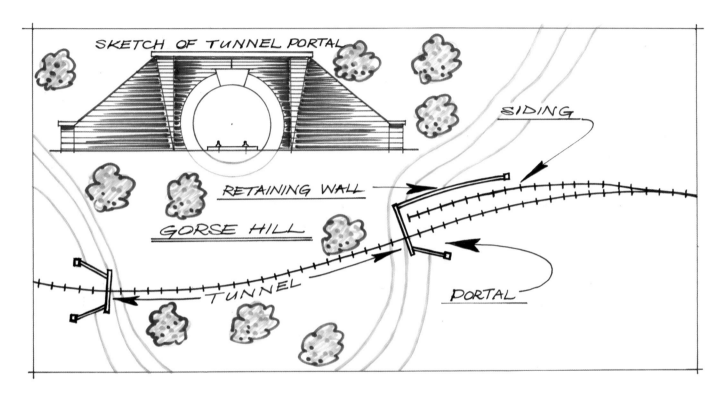

SKETCH OF TUNNEL PORTAL

SIDING

RETAINING WALL

GORSE HILL

TUNNEL

PORTAL

Grandpa filled his old digger with diesel and started it up.

The worn-out engine spluttered into life, making even more smoke than usual. As they drove along to work, Grandpa started day-dreaming. 'With all this money, perhaps I could get the engine rebuilt? Or even buy a new digger!'

Arriving in the field, they started on the earthworks for the tunnel. Grandpa dug while Peter guided him, keeping them to the correct line.

Further and further they nibbled into the hill, with the trench getting deeper and deeper. Eventually the digger could only just lift the earth high enough to drop it on the top.

Every few metres, they hammered another short stake into the ground at the bottom of the trench. They used these to check the height of the track bed with a spirit level, just as they had done on every other piece of line they had built.

At last the trench was dug and they got Mr Beer to come along with the loader, and tip a layer of ballast in the bottom. This would make a good bed to set the pipes onto.

When the pipes arrived, they were very heavy, two tonnes for every metre length. They used the digger as a crane to lift them, but its tyres squashed almost flat. "Oh dear," smiled Grandpa. "I guess we'll have to pump them up a bit!"

Very carefully, they transported the sections of pipe to the trench and laid them down, end to end. Peter kept well out of the way of the heavy pipes while they were being lowered in. After that, it was a simple job to use the digger to push all the soil back in, and cover up the pipes.

In a few more days the tunnel was finished, but it did look an awful mess. There was a wide brown scar right across the field. "I'll scatter some grass seed over it this evening," said Grandpa, half to himself. "That will make it look better for the grand opening."

Peter, meanwhile, was investigating the tunnel from the inside; he could just walk through without banging his head. Once in the middle, it was completely dark and made funny echoing sounds when he clapped his hands. 'I can't wait to drive a train through here,' he thought to himself.

Meeting at one end, they discussed how to build the brick entrance portals.

"I think we shall have to get the local builders in," decided Grandpa. "They will make a better job of it, and much quicker too."

"You're right," agreed Peter. "It will free us up to get on with another good project, The Bridge on the River Wye!"

Constructing the Tunnel

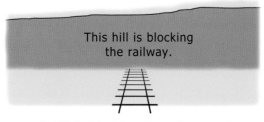

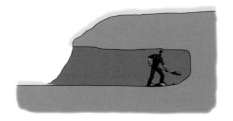

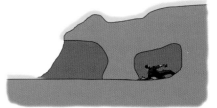

A hill is blocking the railway and a tunnel is needed to get through.

The problem is to dig the tunnel in a safe and simple way.

You might imagine that Peter and Grandpa would dig the tunnel underground, by hand. This would be very dangerous because the roof of the tunnel could easily collapse and bury them under tons of earth.

Tunnelling by the 'Cut and Cover' method

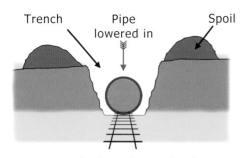

Trench   Pipe lowered in   Spoil

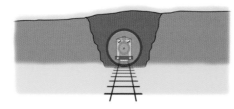

A trench has been 'cut' right through the hill. This is safe because there is no tunnel roof to fall in.

The 'spoil' which has been dug from the trench is dumped at the top.

Once the trench has been cut, the pipe (blue), which forms the tunnel wall, is lowered in.

The trench is now filled in again, using the original soil and the pipe has been covered over.

The pipe which forms the tunnel must be strong enough to support the weight of the earth above it. This has been calculated very carefully, with a large safety margin.

This old picture shows the London Underground being built in 1861. For shallow lines, they dug up the streets and built the tunnels, before covering them over. It must have caused chaos!

Tunnelling Machines
For deeper tunnels, a different method is needed.

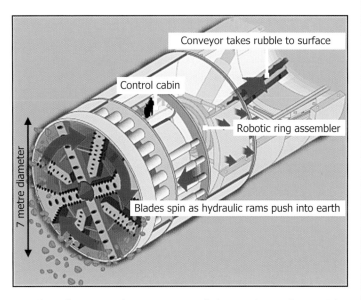

Conveyor takes rubble to surface

Control cabin

Robotic ring assembler

7 metre diameter

Blades spin as hydraulic rams push into earth

This is a photograph of a tunnel boring machine (TBM) just before it starts work, boring the London Crossrail tunnels. It is obvious that they are very large, complex and expensive machines.

You can see from the size of the men, that it is enormous: the length is 150 metres and it weighs 1000 tonnes.

This machine (called Phyllis) can bore up to 150 metres of tunnel in a week, and the position of the tunnel in the ground will be accurate to about 1 mm.

The TBM bores the tunnel and assembles the inside tunnel wall.

This diagram shows a tunnel borer in action. The rotating blades can cut through the ground while a conveyor belt takes the rubble away to the surface.

Hydraulic rams push the rotating cutter forwards, into the ground, with enormous force so that it can cut.

The clever part of the machine is that it holds the tunnel up while it is working, and then assembles wall panels or sections, to make a strong and waterproof tunnel wall. This is done by the robotic ring assembler.

Tunnel boring machines are fantastically expensive, so it's incredible that, often when the tunnel is finished, the machine is left buried underground - entombed. It digs another short tunnel off to the side, where it is abandoned. This can be cheaper than recovering a massive and worn-out machine.

The Bridge on the River Wye

With the builders finishing off the tunnel, it was time to think about the bridge. This was another good project which Peter and Grandpa wanted to do themselves.

After a pleasant walk across the fields, they were looking at the river and discussing how best to cross it. "We will build a simple arch bridge," Grandpa told Peter.

"The beauty of an arch is that its strength comes from the banks of the river, on either side. The load on top of the arch tries to flatten it and push the ends outwards. But as long as the ends can't move apart, the arch is strong and won't fall down."

"We'll have to build a brick abutment on each side first," he explained. "The abutments are the foundations for the bridge. It doesn't matter how hard the arch pushes out against them, they won't budge."

Peter wanted to know how they would build the arch.

"Once we've built the abutments," Grandpa told him, "we'll build a wooden framework or template. It will have a curved top, the shape of the arch, onto which we can lay the bricks. When the cement has set solid, we will remove the framework from underneath."

"And hope the arch stays up!" grinned Peter.

The first job was to dig a big slot in each of the grassy banks. The abutments would be built into these slots.

They took a trailer load of bricks, sand and cement to the construction site. "At least we've got a supply of water for mixing up the cement," they joked.

The next couple of days passed quickly, mixing up concrete to make a base, and then building the two brick abutments. They left a step in the sides, so that the arch itself could find a firm grip.

Then they constructed the temporary wooden framework to support the arch, while it was being built.

Made from wood, it was formed by screwing down some sheets of plywood in a graceful curve.

Finally, they put on some edging strips to keep the side bricks in straight lines. At last the template was ready.

The next day, they mixed up some more cement and started laying the bricks for the arch. First one layer and then a second, curving up and over the river.

After letting the cement go hard for a few days, they built the bridge up to a flat top and finished it off with little walls at either side.

As they were packing up for the day, Cato and Minnie appeared through the trees. They ran back and forwards over the river, inspecting the new bridge. Then, as if to give it their seal of approval, they sat on the ends of the walls, like mascots in the sun.

"They make it look very grand," said Peter, pointing at the animals. "Perhaps we should put statues there, to celebrate our work!"

"It's a good idea," laughed Grandpa. "But we've already got enough to do if we're going to finish this railway on time."

"But you have reminded me of a most interesting bridge at Crewe," he remembered.

"Crewe was one of the greatest locomotive factories in the world and, as it expanded, they needed to build a railway bridge across part of the works."

"It just so happened that in a pile of scrap metal, there were four huge cast-iron eagles. They were going to be melted down in the blast furnace, but the men decided to save them and fixed them onto the ends of the bridge. It was known from then on as the Eagle Bridge."

"There's now a medical clinic where the Works used to be," finished Grandpa. "It's called the Eagle Bridge Health Centre and one of the old eagles is on a plinth just outside."

"That's a good story," said Peter. "But why did they have a blast furnace and steel works at a factory for making locomotives? Surely they would have bought their iron and steel from a steel company?"

"You are thinking of how things are today," replied Grandpa. "Yes, modern factories don't make everything, they usually just assemble parts bought in from other factories."

"But in the old days, machines were much simpler and factories often made absolutely everything, including their own iron and steel."

"In fact," he added, "the railway works were really the first places to make high quality steel. There wasn't anywhere else to buy it from."

"There's a fabulous picture of a locomotive made at Crewe, in 1897. It shows the just-finished engine and, stacked in front, all the raw materials the works had used to make it. They literally started with coal and scrap iron at one end of the factory, and a complete locomotive rolled out of the other end."

"We'll find the picture when we get back to the house," finished Grandpa as they set off across the fields.

A week later, with the cement properly set, they were back at their bridge. It was time to take out the wooden framework. Would the arch stay up?

"Don't get underneath," warned Grandpa. "It wouldn't be funny if it fell down, especially if you got hurt."

With hammers, screwdrivers and saws, they slowly dismantled the support and pulled the wood out, bit by bit.

There wasn't a crack, creak, groan or sag. The bridge held firm.

"Considering nothing happened," laughed Peter, "that was very exciting!"

The two engineers stood on their bridge, thoroughly pleased with themselves.

A wonderful publicity photograph, taken by the London & North Western Railway in 1897 of one of their brand new three cylinder freight locomotives. In front are all the materials they needed to build an engine. The factory at Crewe were very proud of the fact that they made almost everything themselves. They didn't buy finished wheels, boilers and pistons etc. from other factories. They started with raw materials like ingots of copper, scrap iron, limestone, tin and coke.

Arch Bridge

Arch bridges have been in use since before Roman times; the oldest existing arch is in Greece and is over 3000 years old. They are a simple but clever design that enables large bridges to be made with readily available materials. The way the arch gets its strength is explained below.

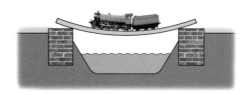

An easy way to put a bridge across a river would be to use a wooden plank (yellow).

To make a proper job, it could be supported on some brick foundations.

A bridge is sometimes called a 'span'.

Unfortunately the plank or beam is not rigid enough and it bends in the middle when a load is put on it.

This might be fine for walking across a small river, but for engineers it is not much of a solution!

To make the bridge stiffer and stronger, a very thick plank or beam could be used.

At least this now works, but it is expensive because it uses a lot of material. It is also difficult to transport such a heavy beam to the site.

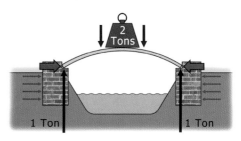

Here, the plank has been bent upwards into an arch shape.

The supports now have a step in them to stop the ends of the arch spreading outwards.

The supports could now be called the 'abutments' for the bridge.

If the top of the arch is forced downwards, it tries to spread outwards and become wider, (the plank stays the same length.)

The abutments prevent the ends from spreading wider and this is what holds the arch up.

You can try this for yourself with a ruler.

If a weight of 2 tons is placed on the bridge, the foundations or abutments will exert an upward force of 1 ton at each end of the arch (black arrows).

To stop the arch flattening and spreading out, the abutments exert a large sideways (inwards) force on the ends of the arch (purple arrows).

To stop the abutments being pushed outwards by the arch (which is trying to flatten and spread out), the ground exerts a large force inwards on the abutments (red arrows).

Brick and Stone Arches

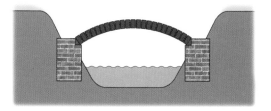

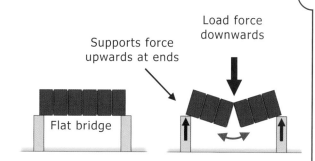

Supports force upwards at ends

Load force downwards

Flat bridge

Peter and Grandpa have built the arch for their bridge from bricks (blue) and cement or 'mortar' (red).

Bricks and mortar are very strong when being pressed together. They are strong in 'compression', so are good materials to construct an arch.

Cement is a very poor glue if you try to pull the bricks apart. It is weak in 'tension'.

Luckily, in an arch the forces are always pressing the bricks and cement together. This stops the bricks from splitting away from each other.

If you were to build a flat bridge (not arched) with bricks and cement, it would certainly fail.

The forces acting on the bridge put the bricks and cement in tension, along the lower edge. The forces are trying to pull the bricks apart.

Cement is a poor glue and it will simply split.

(You can try this as an experiment with 'Lego' bricks, which are strong when pressed together but come apart when pulled. Your bridge should have the bricks on their sides, resting on supports at the ends. Press down in the middle.)

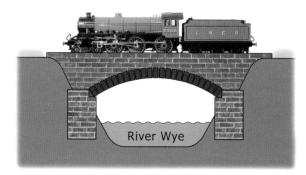

Carrbridge in Scotland

The remains of this old bridge show a simple arch. You can almost see the forces holding it up!

Stoddard Bridge in America

This twin arch bridge is so carefully made that it does not even appear to need cement between the stones. It is held up entirely by compression forces, pushing the stones together.

Peter and Grandpa's bridge

The bridge is finished by building up with bricks (pale blue) to make a flat top for the track.

All the strength is in the curved arch. The top bricks are quite weak and are held up by the arch (dark blue).

The Hydro-Electric Train

One of the things which Peter and Grandpa had done before the summer holidays was to design the new passenger train.

First, our two engineers had to specify what the new train would be like.

"There are 37 children who want to travel on it," began Peter. "And then there is me as the driver, oh yes, and Edward Coni too."

"We can't forget young Edward," agreed Grandpa quickly. "Otherwise his dad might want his land back!"

"So we had better design the train for at least 40 children," decided Peter. "How many carriages are we going to need?"

To decide this important question, they measured out a space on the floor which was 2.5 metres long, or one eighth of the length of a full size railway coach. Then Peter sat on the floor to work out how many children they could fit in each carriage.

"I reckon," said Grandpa after taking a few more measurements, "we should be able to fit in four or five children. If we get 10 carriages, then there should be plenty of room."

They also had to decide how wide and high the carriages should be. The children needed to be able to sit down inside them, to get some shelter from bad weather. However, if they were too high, they would be top heavy and unstable, and might tip over.

There was a lot to think about and they kept adding to the list of requirements.

"We need to have space to put all the school bags," suggested Peter.

"And you need to be able to drive it from either end of the train, as we don't have space at Oaksted for a turning loop," added Grandpa. "With a cab and controls at both ends, you'll simply be able to drive the train backwards for the return trip."

It was time to do a sketch of what one of the carriages would look like, with basic dimensions and how the passengers would fit in.

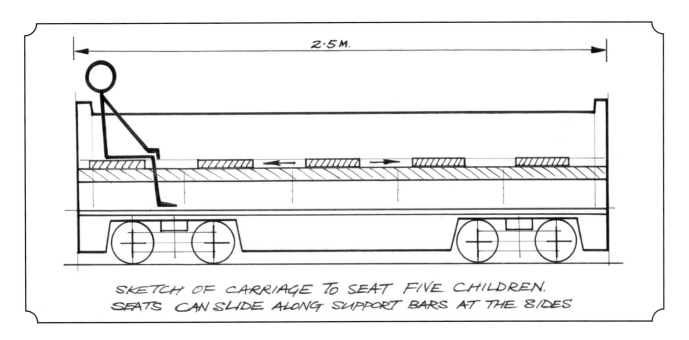

SKETCH OF CARRIAGE TO SEAT FIVE CHILDREN.
SEATS CAN SLIDE ALONG SUPPORT BARS AT THE SIDES

They then started to work out a rough design for the electric locomotive.

"We know it's going to be battery powered," began Grandpa. "But just at the moment it's difficult to work out how large the batteries will have to be. It all depends on how much electricity the motors are going to use."

"I think at this stage in the design, we will have to make an estimate."

"Where do we start?" asked Peter. "We don't really know anything at all!"

"We do know one thing," suggested Grandpa. "We know that with one battery, our little engine Quicksilver runs for about 10 miles."

"We'll need to do two round trips with the school train every day," said Peter, trying to work it out in his head. "Each round trip is going to be 12 miles, so we will need to run about 24 miles between charges."

To add to the problem, the new train would be about 10 times heavier than Quicksilver, and it would also go much faster.

"I think it will need at least four batteries and maybe up to eight," said Grandpa, after doing a few more simple calculations. "It would be better to have too many batteries, rather than too few. I'm sure you don't want to run out of charge, half way home on a dark night."

Luckily, Peter hit on the solution. "If we plan to put four batteries in the engine, and a space for me to sit and drive," he suggested. "Then we could just do the same at the other end: four more batteries and space for me to drive when running the other way."

"That's it," agreed Grandpa instantly. "And, if we set the batteries really low down, there will be space above them for all the school bags and stuff."

"Big batteries are seriously heavy," he added. "They will keep the centre of gravity low, so it won't have a chance of tipping over."

Now they could do a sketch of the driving car or locomotive. There would be one at each end of the train.

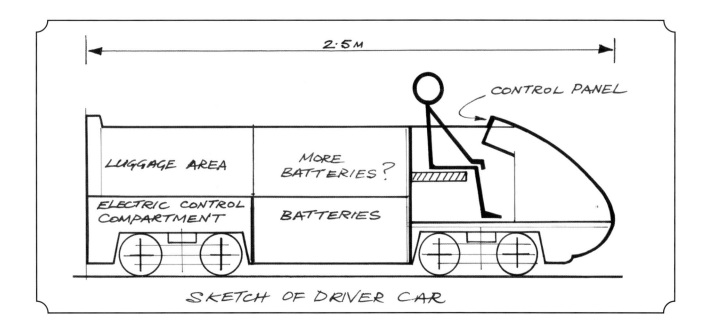

SKETCH OF DRIVER CAR

With the deadline of opening the railway by the end of the holidays, there simply wasn't time for Peter and Grandpa to build the train themselves. They would have to pay an engineering company to make it for them.

They did more drawings and added extra information and requirements. They specified the tightest radius or curve of the track, the steepest gradients and the top speed the train would have to go - 20 miles per hour! All this information would allow engineers to work out the sizes of the motors and electrical control gear. Also specified were a speedometer, automatic brakes, a loud horn and very bright headlights, so the train could be driven in the dark.

It had taken a while to find an engineering company to make the train. But at last they had found Colpoys Engineering, who quoted a sensible price for the job and agreed to work out all the details from the specifications.

Today, two months later, the new train was being delivered. Peter and Grandpa were waiting in the farm yard for the lorry to arrive.

"That is some lorry!" said Peter as it came up the road. "It's even got a crane to unload everything."

Grandpa directed the lorry to park beside the railway, so that the engines and carriages could be lowered straight onto the line.

"Good morning to you," said Mr Colpoys, jumping down from the cab and shaking Peter and Grandpa by the hand. "I thought I would come over myself and show you exactly how it all works. I also wanted to see your grand railway project."

One by one, the carriages were lowered onto the track.

There were two locomotives, one for each end. As the crane took the load, it was clear from the hissing hydraulics that they were very heavy. "We've installed four massive batteries in each," explained Mr Colpoys. "They are full of lead, which is why each loco unit weighs nearly half a tonne!"

Mr Colpoys showed them how to couple everything together.

"We haven't used chains and hooks," he explained. "If one carriage comes off the track, a chain would allow it to tip over and wreck the whole train."

"Instead there are slots with steel plates and locking pins. They will allow the train to bend round curves, but they don't let one carriage tip over."

Then he showed them how to connect the brake pipes and all the

electric cables between the carriages. "This one is the main power supply. And this multi-pin connector is for horn, lights and control wires," he told them. "It's quite complicated because you wanted to be able to drive it from either end."

Lifting up a small hatch on the roof of one of the engines, he showed them another electrical socket. "This is where you plug in the charger," he explained. "You only have to plug it in at one end, and both locomotives will be charged at the same time."

"I have added one thing to your specification," Mr Colpoys continued, "Regenerative brakes. This means that when you put the brakes on, the electronic control circuits use the motors as generators to put electricity back into the batteries."

"Old fashioned brakes use friction to slow the train down, and turn all the motion energy into wasted heat. With these modern brakes, most of the motion energy is recovered."

"Would you like to test it out now?" he asked with a big grin.

Once Peter had been shown all the controls in the cab, he climbed in and snuggled down. It was comfy inside but not very large.

"You can drive forwards at full speed from either end," said Mr Colpoys. "But you can only go backwards at slow speed, for manoeuvring. If you want to go fast the other way, you will have to get in the other end, so you can see where you are going!"

Peter released the brakes and moved the power lever to the forward position, slow. With a quiet, high pitched whining noise from the electronics and motors, the train moved off. Then he tried the slow reverse and motored back.

"We had better take it for a test run round our original line," suggested Grandpa to Mr Colpoys. "I think we can squeeze into a carriage, but we should load the others up with bricks to act as a test load."

As you can imagine, they spent the rest of the day trying out the new train. With each circuit of the track, Peter became more confident and drove a little faster.

Brakes - Friction and Regenerative

Friction brakes

Friction brakes are the normal type of brakes and they are found nearly everywhere. Bicycles have them, most cars and trains have them.

Friction brakes work by rubbing some sort of brake block or pad against a moving wheel or disc.

Friction converts the energy of movement into heat energy. Unfortunately it isn't possible to re-use, or recover, this heat energy and so it is wasted.

Regenerative brakes

Energy is expensive and should not be wasted. So it would be a good idea to try to recover the energy which is lost in the brakes of a car, bicycle or train.

In an electric vehicle, it is possible to use the motor in reverse as an electric generator.

The motor, instead of driving the wheels, is now being driven by them and slowing them down. It is braking the train and generating electricity at the same time.

Stopped

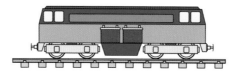

Train with friction brakes

Stopped at beginning of its journey. The batteries are fully charged (red).

No power (electricity) is being used yet.

Stopped

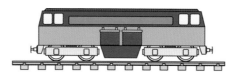

Train with regenerative brakes

Exactly the same as above. The train is stopped at beginning of its journey. The batteries are fully charged (red).

Accelerating

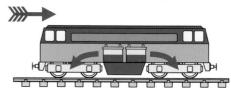

Working hard

The locomotive is now accelerating and pulling hard on the train.

The electric motors are drawing a lot of power from the batteries and using up a lot of their stored electricity.

Electrical energy is being converted to motion ('kinetic') energy of the train.

Accelerating

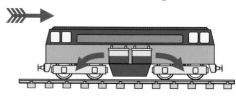

Working hard

Same as above. The traction motors are drawing a large electric current from the batteries, to accelerate the train.

The energy in the batteries is being converted to kinetic or motion energy of the train.

Full size trains. Modern electric trains have regenerative brakes, but they put the recovered energy or electricity back into the overhead power line. It can then be used by other trains and reduces the cost of electricity for the railways.

Saving Energy and Electricity

Running

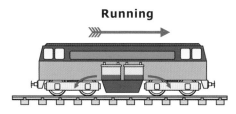

Fast but steady speed

The locomotive is now running along the line.

The electric motors are drawing less power to keep the train moving. Electricity is still being used from the batteries.

Friction braking

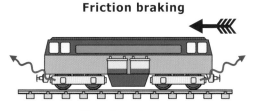

Slowing down

Friction brake pads or shoes are now rubbing on the wheels or disc brakes, to slow the train down.

All the motion (kinetic) energy in the train is being wasted by turning it into heat. The brakes are getting hot.

Stopped

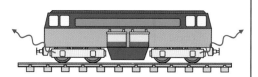

Wasted energy

The train has stopped and the brakes are cooling down, giving all their heat energy to the surrounding air.

No energy has been put back into the batteries. It has been wasted.

Running

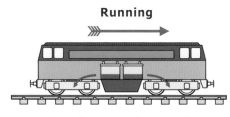

Fast but steady speed

Same as above. The motors and batteries are working to keep the train moving.

The energy is being used to overcome air-resistance (drag) and friction in the wheels and bearings.

Regenerative braking

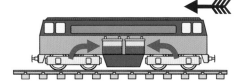

Slowing down, recovering energy

Now the traction motors are being used as generators to put electrical energy back into the batteries.

The kinetic energy of the train is being converted into electrical energy to recharge the batteries.

Stopped

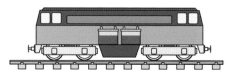

Batteries recharged - a bit.

Compared to the friction brakes above, the regenerative brakes have saved a lot of energy to leave the batteries with more charge.

The batteries will take less energy to recharge at night.

Electric cars always have regenerative brakes to put the recovered energy back into their batteries. This increases the distance they can drive, before the batteries are flat. The limited range of electric cars is the reason why they are not more popular.

Hollow Tree Halt

The bridge and tunnel were finished, the train had been delivered and the men were levelling up the track for a smooth line. But there were still a few jobs left. Peter and Grandpa wanted to make sure everything was perfect before they wrote to the Minister and invited him to open the line.

"We still have to put in a platform and shelter for young Edward Coni," said Peter as they looked at the list of things to do.

"That's most important," agreed Grandpa. "It was part of the deal we did with his dad. Let's make that our next job."

They coupled a few trucks onto Quicksilver and set off down the line to Woodland Cottage and then walked across the fields to Bean Farm. The workmen had already put down a little platform of paving slabs, right next to a hollow old oak tree. The problem was that this tree was exactly where the station building should be.

They were wondering what to do about it when Grandpa started to laugh. "We'll build the station in the hollow tree," he declared. "It will be just like they did at the village of Moreton-on-Lugg."

"In about 1850, the Shrewsbury and Hereford Railway was being built. There were two gigantic oak trees, called Adam and Eve, just beside the line," he explained. "Adam had been blown down in a storm and Eve had its top blown off, leaving a large hollow stump."

"The railway company was very concerned about costs and so, to save money, they converted Eve into a station, with a thatched roof over the gaping top!"

"You are joking," said Peter, looking very dubious.

"Not at all," replied Grandpa. "These trees were bigger than you think. A party of fifteen once drank tea inside one of them and twenty one sheep could take shelter in the other. Eve became the station house and office for the first Station Master, and I think this old oak tree, beside our line, will make a perfect station for young Edward."

"We'll trim up the top of the tree, at a slight angle," explained Grandpa. "Then we can nail a tin roof on the top, to keep the rain out."

Grandpa, whose mind often went off in funny directions, then told Peter about the metal, tin. "Did you know that in the old days, it was used to protect steel, to stop it from rusting. But being expensive, it is only used for food containers nowadays; that is why they are called tins!"

"There is one really useful thing I can tell you about tin," continued Grandpa. "And it will be handy when you study chemistry at school one day. You'll have to learn all the symbols for the different chemical elements. Most of them are simple to remember: C for carbon, S for sulphur, H for hydrogen and so on. But tin is difficult, its symbol is Sn."

"But when I was at school," he smiled, "I devised a cunning method to remember it by. First you have to know that there was a very famous poet called Alfred Lord Tennyson. Then you just think of him as 'Lord Tin SN', and you'll never forget."

"That's terrible," groaned Peter. "But you are right, I won't forget it now, even if I wanted to!"

The two friends then got back to the job of converting the old tree. After returning with tools and materials, they trimmed off the top and nailed on the roof. There was no need to make a doorway because there was a hole in the side of the trunk, between the gnarled old roots. It was big enough for a small person to walk through.

They made a bench seat inside from some planks of wood, and then two more seats on the platform, cut from solid oak.

Finally, Peter made and painted a sign and fixed it to a couple of posts. "Hollow Tree Halt". Edward was going to love his station.

There were still some jobs to do, but with only a few weeks left of the holidays, it was time to write to the Minister of Transport.

That evening they wrote a letter, inviting him to come and open the railway. With great glee, they put it in an envelope, together with the bill or invoice for building the line. It was from a company called PR Construction Ltd. and was for £5 million!

Jackpot!

Monday morning was a perfectly ordinary Monday morning for the Minister of Transport. He was sitting in his big leather chair at his huge mahogany desk in his enormous office in London. His secretary Alex had put a pile of papers and letters in front of him and he was working his way through them.

This document needed signing, that transport policy needed a review, an order for new pencils here, a proposal for hydrogen-powered buses there. A hand-written letter...

He started reading and the colour drained from his face.

"Oh dear!" he muttered to himself. "It was only a crazy suggestion from a schoolboy and his old grandpa. I never thought they would actually build their railway!"

Then he saw the next piece of paper, the bill from PR Construction Limited.

Picking it up, he could only see the total amount at the end. "FIVE MILLION POUNDS!!" he read aloud. His hands started to shake and he broke into a cold sweat.

'Whatever shall I do? The accountants will go nuts. I know I agreed to it. We will have to pay. My career will be ruined!' All these thoughts whirled round inside the Minister of Transport's head.

After a few minutes of blind panic, the Minister calmed himself down and read the letter again, this time to the end.

"Thank you so much for your support in this project," Peter's letter finished, "we are really looking forward to your visit to open the line."

"PS. All my friends from school are very excited about appearing with you on TV!"

Dropping the letter, the Minister leapt out of his chair, smiling. He had forgotten all about the television programme.

"Thank goodness for that," he said aloud. "Everything is going to be just fine."

"Alex!" he shouted through to his secretary. "Telephone the Director General of the BBC. Tell him to organize a film crew for the opening of the Oaksted Railway!"

"Oh yes, and tell the accountants to write out a cheque to pay PR Construction Limited. I'll sign it this afternoon."

Quite exhausted from all this activity, he sat down again. '£5 million of taxpayers' money isn't very much,' he smiled to himself, 'especially if it makes me look good on TV!'

A few days later, the postman delivered a letter to Crossacres Farm. It was addressed to Peter, who opened it with trembling hands. It contained a letter and a cheque.

Peter read the letter first. It explained that the Minister of Transport would like to attend the opening ceremony on the last day of the holiday, together with the television crew to film the new train and children riding in it. He would arrive by train at Oaksted mainline station, at 2.00 pm.

Then, looking at the cheque, Peter could hardly believe his eyes. Not saying a word (because he was speechless!), he passed it over to his grandparents.

Suddenly everyone was talking at once. "You've really hit the jackpot now!" "I have never seen so many zeros on a cheque." "You had better pay it into the bank at once." "Quickly, before he changes his mind!"

There was still time to get to the bank in Yockletts before closing time. So Peter and Grandpa rushed outside, coupled some wagons behind Quicksilver, and set off at the double. Arriving at the river, they ran across the bridge, and into the bank.

"Come to pay in your pocket money, Sonny?" asked the bank manager, looking through his glasses on the end of his nose.

"No. I'd like to pay in this cheque for PR Construction please," replied Peter politely, pushing it through the slot.

The bank manager was so surprised, his glasses fell off. He had never seen a cheque for £5 million before. And certainly not one being presented by a small boy!

On the way home, Grandpa told Peter that they would ask Grandma to write out cheques to pay every single one of their bills. "For the land, the rails, train, fencing, everything. Then we can really start to enjoy ourselves," he finished.

"Will there be anything left?" Peter asked rather nervously.

"Don't you worry about that!" laughed Grandpa. "You'll have plenty!"

The two friends, engineers and conspirators enjoyed their run back up the line to Crossacres Farm.

The Oaksted Railway

The last day of the summer holidays dawned bright and sunny. Grandma had been up early, cooking cakes for a gigantic tea. With the children from school, their parents, a film crew and a Government Minister, this was going to be her biggest party ever.

Peter and Grandpa were up early too. They were busy lighting Mighty Atom's fire and oiling her up, ready for her important duty. They were using their old traction engine to collect the Minister from Oaksted railway station.

Her boiler was just starting to sing and sizzle, when a car arrived. It was Mr Esmond, who had built Fiery Fox. He had come over for the day, to help out.

"Hello!" he greeted his friends. "You've got a perfect day to open a new railway."

"I'll look after Fiery Fox while you two concentrate on everything else. You can't just leave a small steam engine on its own. Either the fire will go out, or the water level will get low and the boiler might explode."

"Neither of those events would look good on television!" agreed Grandpa quickly.

At midday, Peter and Grandpa coupled up a trailer behind Mighty Atom, threw on a couple of bales of straw, and set off down the road for Oaksted. They were leaving in plenty of time as they didn't want to be late.

It was a splendid trip, with Mighty Atom bowling along at a steady 7 miles an hour, chuffing and clanking her old gears. Some car drivers pulled over to one side and waited for them to pass, while others didn't seem to notice them at all. One old lady pulled so far into the bank at the side of the road, that she nearly tipped her car onto its roof. They gave her a cheery Peep Peep on the whistle to thank her!

Waiting at the station, they oiled around the motion again, ready for the journey home. At two o'clock on the dot, the Minister's train rolled in and he jumped down.

"Hello, hello!" he greeted them. "It's so lovely to get out of London for the day. Are we going to your farm on the new train?"

"That would be a bit difficult," replied Grandpa, shaking his hand, "because you haven't opened the line yet! We thought we would give you a ride behind our old traction engine."

The Minister of Transport, in his very smart pale blue suit, climbed up onto the trailer and sat himself down on a bale of straw. Peter and Grandpa jumped onto the engine and drove out of the station car park and down the road. As usual, Grandpa was in charge of the engine and brakes, while Peter was steering.

'I wonder how many laws we are breaking?' the Minister wondered to himself. 'I don't think small boys are allowed to drive steam engines on the road. And there certainly isn't a seat belt on this bale of straw!' Luckily he kept his thoughts to himself and just hoped they didn't see any policemen on the journey.

The film crew from the BBC were on the lawn, in front of Woodland Cottage, when they arrived.

The Minister tried to look serious, but this was not easy to do, sitting on a bale of straw. His suit had also acquired some large and grubby patches of oil and soot from Mighty Atom's chimney.

"Welcome to Peter's Railway," proclaimed Grandpa in a loud but friendly voice. "We hope you have a very enjoyable day here."

"Before we open the new line," he continued, "we are going to take you on a tour of our old line, behind the steam engine Fiery Fox. You can ride in Grandma's Special Saloon Carriage."

"We call it the Granny Wagon," added Peter. "But not when she's within earshot!"

Mr Esmond had the train all ready. Steam was up and the fire was burning bright and hot. Peter climbed onto the engine and the Minister climbed into the Granny Wagon. Some children clambered on too.

As they steamed out of the station, the Minister found himself wondering again if it was legal for small boys to drive steam trains, especially with a Minister of State on board.

Leaving the station at Woodland Cottage, the line wound its way through the trees in the orchard and then ran along beside the River Woe. Peter stopped the train at their watermill so they could show the Minister where they generated hydro-electricity.

"You mean to say that you built all this out of scrap bits and pieces?" the Minister asked, amazed. "The government would have paid millions of pounds to build this!"

Back on the train, they set off across the field, towards Bluebell Wood and Crossacres farmhouse. Not stopping, Peter drove on towards Yockletts village, down the long gradient to their little station by the river.

Meanwhile, back at Woodland Cottage, Mr Esmond was positioning the new train on the turning loop, in the trees, out of sight.

After a short stop at Yockletts station, Peter took the steam train slowly round the loop, then he opened the regulator fully and charged the bank. Sparks flew from the chimney as Fiery Fox roared up the hill, faster and faster. They tore back through the station at Crossacres, flashed past the duck pond, and soon were back at Woodland Cottage.

"I never knew a small engine could go so fast," grinned the Minister, stepping out of the Granny Wagon. "What's next?"

Grandpa showed him the junction where the new Oaksted line branched off. A ribbon was tied across the end of the new track, ready for the opening ceremony.

While Grandpa and the Minister were talking, Peter and his school friends crept away and climbed aboard the new train. With a loud 'Beep-Barp' on the horn, Peter drove slowly out from the trees, and stopped at the ribbon, headlights blazing.

The crowd gasped and gathered round. The Minister smiled proudly, it was better than anything he could have imagined.

"I would like to thank the Minister of Transport..." Grandpa addressed the crowd, "...for all his help and support in building our new railway. I now invite him, officially, to open the Oaksted Extension."

With the crowd and cameras watching, the Minister stepped forward, looking very important.

"It gives me great pleasure... and pride... to open the Oaksted Railway," he began. "It is a fine example to the rest of the country... indeed to the world... of how to reduce transport pollution and still provide an essential service."

"I now pronounce the Oaksted Green Extension, Open!" And he cut the ribbon with a pair of sheep shears, which Grandpa had provided for the occasion.

With another loud blast on the horn, Peter drove slowly through the ribbon, with the children on the train cheering and waving flags as they glided past.

The Minister inspected the train and asked all sorts of good questions, but soon it was time for the first run up the line.

"If you would like to sit in the power car at the rear of the train," Peter offered, "you'll get a splendid view of the line. Just don't fiddle with any of the controls!"

Peter got back into the front of the train and drove slowly up the new line. Everyone was waving as they set off towards Oaksted.

For a few yards they ran slowly through the dark trees and then, in bright sunshine, Peter accelerated as the line ran across a field. A moment later, they plunged into the tunnel.

It was pitch black inside and all the children screamed with delight. The Minister of Transport had a grin from ear to ear, but he was glad that no one could see it.

Shooting out of the tunnel, they sped across field after field and past Hollow Tree Halt. The electric train surged along, with nothing but the humming and whining of its electric motors to indicate the great power of the machine.

Approaching the bridge, Peter slowed right down so they could enjoy the view. As he put the brakes on, the electronics made a different sort of whining sound while the motors worked in reverse. They were putting the energy of the moving train back into the batteries.

The view from the bridge was spectacular, with the water rushing underneath, but Peter was soon accelerating again. The power saved from the last brake application was being used to speed them up!

At last, Oaksted Station came into view in the distance. Peter eased off the power and their speed started to drop away. They came to rest at the buffer stops at the end of the line.

After posing for some photographs, Peter and the Minister swapped ends and they set off again, to try out the school run. This time they charged all the way up the line, arriving at Yockletts just 20 minutes later. It was quicker than using a car on the winding country roads.

Fiery Fox had followed them from Woodland Cottage, bringing the film crew and all their equipment. With the children gathered round, the Minister spoke to the television camera.

"This splendid new train," he began, "will save over 5000 gallons of fuel every year. I would like to express my admiration and thanks to all the young people who have worked so hard to turn a dream into reality."

"I am proud," he finished, "to have been able to help by funding such a worthwhile project. Thank you!"

Then the film crew asked if it would be possible to film some high speed running with both the new train and Fiery Fox. "It will look really good in the film," they explained.

In one shot, they had the new train rushing out of the tunnel with Fiery Fox steaming along beside it on the siding. It was then that Grandpa saw one of the children on the track.

Putting the brakes on he stopped quickly. "I know this is only a small train," he said kindly, "but you really must be more careful."

"And just so you don't ever forget, I'm going to tell you a true story."

Can you see a (deliberate) mistake in this picture? The answer is hidden somewhere in this book.

"About a hundred and fifty years ago," he began, "a driver called Nottman was steaming along the line between Dumfries and Carlisle, in Scotland. Looking ahead, he suddenly saw a child on the line. Incredibly, the child was asleep with his head on the rail!"

"Nottman slammed on the brakes, flung the engine into reverse, and shrieked with the whistle. But it was hopeless. The child was fast asleep in the sun and they would never stop in time."

"Driver Nottman climbed out of his cab and, holding onto the handrails, he ran along the side of his engine to the front."

"Then in great danger to himself and holding on as best he could, he climbed down and held one foot just above the rail."

"The train was slowing down now and, as the front wheel was just about to hit the poor child, Nottman, ever so gently, just pushed him to safety with his foot."

"Was he alright?" the children wanted to know. They were horrified at the story.

"Amazingly he was only slightly scratched," smiled Grandpa. "And even more amazing than that, it turned out that the child was the driver's own little boy!"

"He had gone down to the line to watch his daddy's train go past. He wanted to wave to him, but must have got tired and just sat down for a sleep."

"A little bit of innocent play, so nearly ended in tragedy," said Grandpa seriously, finishing the story. "Just remember, never, ever, play on the full size railways. Modern trains run so fast and silently, that you can be killed before you even hear one approaching."

With the warning over, Grandpa felt a tug at his sleeve. It was Harry and he was so excited, he was jumping up and down.

"Grandpa," he asked. "Can I drive the new electric train? I promise I'll be careful!"

"Of course you can," Grandpa smiled at him. "Why don't you get in one end and Kitty can get in the other. Then you can take it in turns to drive slowly up and down through the station. I'll show you what to do."

With happy grins, Harry and Kitty drove up and down through Yewston station, through the trees and back again.

The only problem was that Harry could not resist pressing the horn button. It was just in front of him and seemed to attract his finger like a magnet. 'BEEP BAAARP,' he went for the hundredth time.

"If you keep beeping the horn," joked Peter, "you'll flatten all the batteries. Then you won't be able to drive any longer!"

With less blowing of the horn, Grandpa was now talking to the Minister. "I do hope you will stay for a celebration tea party, up at the farm," he invited him. "When it's time for you to leave, Peter will run you up the line to Oaksted, so you can catch your train to London."

"Wonderful!" laughed the Minister. "I just hope I'll fit in the little train after eating all the cakes!"

Quite apart from the endless food, the party was a great success. Lots of people made speeches, thanking Peter and Grandpa for building the railway. And, of course, they thanked the Minister for paying for it.

The local band arrived and played, the children sang songs, and a good time was had by all. In fact it was such a good party that no one had noticed how late it was getting.

"Goodness gracious!" exclaimed the Minister suddenly. "I'd completely forgotten about the time and I've missed the last train to London!"

"Don't worry," Peter told him, after whispering quickly with Grandma. "My grandmother will drive you back up to London. I've just bought her a new car as a present, to thank her and Grandpa for all the help they have given me."

Relieved that he would still get back to London, the Minister once again found himself somewhat out of his depth. What was a schoolboy doing, buying a car for his grandmother? How could he afford it? Was it an old banger?

Thanking everyone again, he went outside while Grandma went to get her new car.

The look on his face was one of pure astonishment, as an enormous car purred almost silently into the yard. Grandma was behind the wheel of a brand new Rolls Royce!

"It only arrived from the factory yesterday," explained Peter with a grin. "It's a special version which can run for short distances on electricity from batteries."

"Er... Good gracious," spluttered the Minister, who could hardly speak.

"We can charge it up from our watermill," Peter explained helpfully as the Minister stepped in. "It's another super-green form of transport."

They all said goodbye and Peter closed the door with a soft clunk.

Sitting on the softest leather seat, the poor Minister was itching to know how Peter could afford to buy such a splendid motor car, but he knew it would be rude to ask. At the same time, an uncomfortable thought occurred to him. Had he paid too much for building the new line? And just who owned PR Construction Limited?

Only Grandma guessed what was troubling the Minister of Transport. And she was saying nothing!

The big Rolls Royce crunched across the gravel drive.

The End.

Some Special Words

Abutments   The foundations or strong parts which support the ends of a bridge. They take the forces from the bridge and pass them into the ground. Sometimes called Buttresses.

Accountants   People who keep a record of a company's or person's money. They keep records or 'accounts' of all the money which comes in and goes out.

Bank account   Something which holds money at a bank. The owner or customer of the account can pay money into it or take money out of their account. A sort of grown-up piggy bank.

Companies House   The office where details of all companies are registered, to make them legal.

Contract   An agreement between people or organisations. Usually the contract is signed by all involved so that they have a proper record of what they have agreed.

Cover image
(and page 88)   Did you notice that the tunnel is rather too low? It would be difficult for the Granny Wagon to fit through. The 'deliberate mistake' is so the picture fits on the front cover!

Cutting   Trench dug through a high piece of ground to keep the line level.

Cylinder   Round and smooth tube which contains the piston. The cylinders and pistons are the parts of the locomotive where the energy in the steam is converted into the useful motion of the train.

Embankment   Built-up mound of earth which carries the line over a dip in the ground.

Friction   The resistance to motion when one object slides over another and generates heat.

Gradient   Slope or hill. Usually on railways they are fairly gentle compared to roads.

Hydraulics   The use of very high pressure oil (or water) to operate machines. Either by pushing pistons (called rams in hydraulics) or by turning special motors.

Hydro-electricity   Electricity made from falling or flowing water.

Invoice   Document describing the sale of something. It tells the customer how much to pay.

Jackpot   A large amount of money, won as a prize. 'Hit the jackpot' - win the big prize.

Jig   Simple device or tool to make a repetitive task easier, when making things.

Limited company	A business or company which has limited liability. This means that if they make a bad mistake, the people who own or run the company do not have all their personal money and houses taken away to pay for the mistake.
Lord Tennyson	Famous poet of "Charge of the Light Brigade". Many of his phrases are now commonplace in the English language. Eg "'Tis better to have loved and lost / Than never to have loved at all", "Their's not to reason why, / Their's but to do and die".
Pantograph	Mounted on the roof of an electric train, it picks up electricity from the overhead wire.
Per	Means 'for each'. As in miles per hour (mph), means miles for each hour.
Piston	Round disc which fits perfectly and slides in the cylinder. Steam pushes on the piston to turn the wheels by using the connecting rod and crank.
Points (set of)	Junction between two tracks where trains can be switched from one to the other. Sometimes called Turnouts or, in America, Switches.
Pressure	When a lot of steam is squashed into a closed space, its pressure rises. Pressure is often measured in 'pounds per square inch' (or 'psi' for short).
Public money	See Taxpayers' money.
Regulator	Main steam valve used by the driver to control how much steam is used in the cylinders. The more the regulator is opened, the harder and faster the locomotive works. (The regulator is often called the throttle in America.)
Short circuit	An electrical path in a circuit, usually a fault, which allows the electric current to take a short cut, bypassing the intended load. (The load might be a motor or lamp etc.)
Steam	When water boils it bubbles and turns into steam. Normally steam has a very large volume compared to the water it came from. However, in the boiler it is contained in a closed space and so, instead of expanding to a large volume, it rises in pressure.
Taxpayers' money	Money that governments spend. It is collected from the people of the country who pay tax. It can be used to build roads, run schools and hospitals, pay for the army and police, etc. Also called Public money.
£ sign	The British pound, the unit of money or currency used in Britain or the UK.

The Boiler - How the Locomotive Makes its Steam

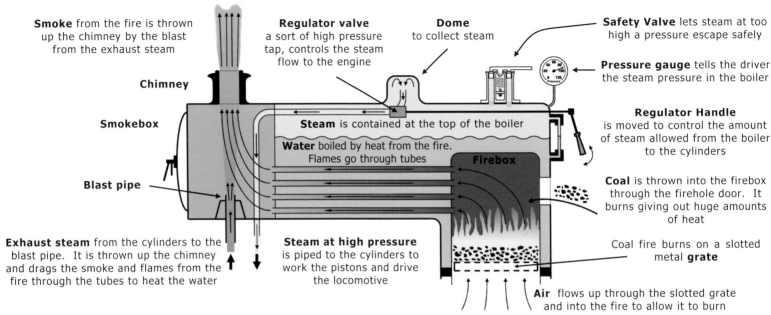

Smoke from the fire is thrown up the chimney by the blast from the exhaust steam

Chimney

Smokebox

Blast pipe

Regulator valve a sort of high pressure tap, controls the steam flow to the engine

Dome to collect steam

Safety Valve lets steam at too high a pressure escape safely

Pressure gauge tells the driver the steam pressure in the boiler

Regulator Handle is moved to control the amount of steam allowed from the boiler to the cylinders

Steam is contained at the top of the boiler

Water boiled by heat from the fire. Flames go through tubes

Firebox

Coal is thrown into the firebox through the firehole door. It burns giving out huge amounts of heat

Coal fire burns on a slotted metal **grate**

Exhaust steam from the cylinders to the blast pipe. It is thrown up the chimney and drags the smoke and flames from the fire through the tubes to heat the water

Steam at high pressure is piped to the cylinders to work the pistons and drive the locomotive

Air flows up through the slotted grate and into the fire to allow it to burn

Pistons and Cylinders - How the Steam Drives the Locomotive

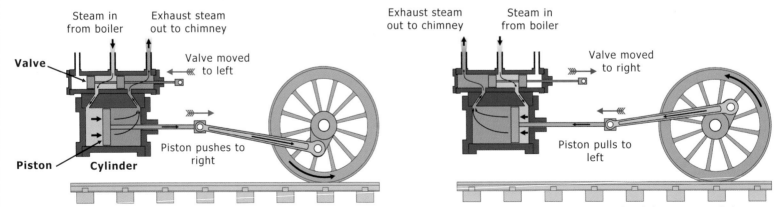

Steam in from boiler

Exhaust steam out to chimney

Exhaust steam out to chimney

Steam in from boiler

Valve

Valve moved to left

Valve moved to right

Piston

Cylinder

Piston pushes to right

Piston pulls to left

The piston pushes and pulls the wheel round with the high pressure steam from the boiler pushing first on one side of the piston and then on the other. The steam is let in and out of alternate ends of the cylinder by the valve which is moved automatically by the valve gear.